Megan – Happy
Mommy – Daddy

W9-AIB-253

BUNNIES
ON THEIR OWN

Pictures by Marie H. Henry
Story by Amy Ehrlich

Dial Books for Young Readers
NEW YORK

For Marie, Cecile, Clara, Helene…
M. H. H.

For my wonderful
friends at Dial
A. E.

First published in the United States 1986 by
Dial Books for Young Readers
A Division of E. P. Dutton
A Division of New American Library
2 Park Avenue
New York, New York 10016
Originally published by Duculot, Paris-Gembloux 1986
Published simultaneously in Canada by
Fitzhenry & Whiteside Limited, Toronto
© 1986 by Duculot Paris-Gembloux
© 1986 by Amy Ehrlich for the American text
All rights reserved

Printed in Belgium by Offset Printing Van den Bossche
Typography by Atha Tehon
First Edition
COBE
10 9 8 7 6 5 4 3 2 1

Library of Congress Cataloging-in-Publication Data
Henry, Marie H.
Bunnies on their own.
Summary: When Mother Bunny goes out, Paulette
decides that she would rather play her bugle than help
her brothers with the cleaning.
[1. Rabbits—Fiction. 2. Brothers and sisters—Fiction.]
I. Ehrlich, Amy, 1942– . II. Title.
PZ7.H395Bw 1986   [E]   85-20467
ISBN 0-8037-0256-6

The art for each picture consists of a watercolor painting,
which is camera-separated and reproduced in full color.

It was marketing day.
Mother Bunny settled her
fur hat around her ears
and went to say good-bye
to her children.

She could hardly believe her eyes. Larry and Harry
were in their room and they were actually playing
quietly.

"Be good little bunnies while I'm gone," she told
them. "Promise me you'll clean up the kitchen.
And don't fight with your sister."

But wait!
Where *was* Paulette?

Up in the attic a
chair scraped across
the floor. . . .

Slowly the attic
window opened. . . .

And a bugle rang out in the rain. *Ta Ta Ta TA!*
"Paulette!" cried Mother Bunny. "What are you
doing up there? Come down this instant!"

"I guess she didn't like my music.

"But I bet Larry and Harry will.

"What's wrong with them? They're practically asleep.

"Wake up, you two! Look what I have!"

Ta Ta Ta TA! Ta Ta Ta TA!
"Owww! Stop, stop!" pleaded the bunny brothers
as they took cover.

"Come on. It didn't sound *that* bad," said Paulette.

"If you want to know how a bugle *should* be played, give me a turn," said Harry.
"Me first," said Larry.

"This is *my* bugle and I'm not going to let you have it," Paulette said.

"That's what you think!" Harry yelled.

Paulette pulled as hard as she could, but it was two against one.

"What a baby you are!" said Larry. "We were only teasing. Who'd want to play your dumb bugle anyway?

"Just leave her alone, Harry. She'll get over it."
And with that the bunny brothers went downstairs to clean up the kitchen.

"Come on, Paulette. You're supposed to help too," said Larry.

If only she could blast them with her bugle and make
them drop all the dishes! But Paulette didn't have
the nerve.

Instead she pretended to help, tiptoeing around the
kitchen and moving spoons from one place to another.

Harry didn't notice but Larry soon caught on.
"If you don't start working, I'm going to tell Mama
on you," he said.

"Come on now. Put the bugle down and take this dish towel."

Paulette had had enough of being bossed around by the bunny brothers. "Me? A dish towel? What for?" she asked innocently.

"Do you want me to be a ghost?

"Or maybe a belly dancer?"

"No," said Larry. "WE WANT
YOU TO DRY THE DISHES!"

"How much more to go? Aren't we almost done?" Paulette complained. "When's Mama coming back anyway?"

"Not till tonight," said Harry. "There's plenty of time."

"Why didn't you say so? I've got better things to do right now. Like PLAY MY BUGLE." And Paulette threw down her dish towel and marched out of the kitchen.

It took Larry and Harry a while to realize she was
actually gone. Then from above their heads came an
unmistakable *Ta Ta Ta TA! Ta Ta Ta TA!*

"Just wait until I get my hands on her!" said Harry.
"Right! This time it's a fight to the finish!" agreed
Larry.

"Come on! She's up here!"

"She's disappeared into thin air," whispered Harry.
"Sssh, be quiet. I think I hear her," whispered Larry.

"This way, Larry, this way.
What are you waiting for!"

Paulette heard her brothers' footsteps. They were
gaining on her. She climbed into Mama's old cupboard
—and not a moment too soon.

Uh-oh! They'd found a clue. "Her slipper!" said
Harry.

"Seize the evidence!" said Larry.

Inside the cupboard Paulette held her breath.

But it was too late.
She'd been discovered.

Those bullies!

How dare they
lock her up!

Oh, well.

She'd think
about it later.

Downstairs Larry and Harry
stopped in their tracks.
"Listen!" said Larry.
"Someone's at the door."

"It's Grandma! Now we're really going to get it!"
"Don't worry," said Larry. "Leave everything to me.
I'll do the talking."

"Oh, hi, Grandma. Mama went shopping and we've been good bunnies all day long and we did the dishes and..."

cookies? That was really nice of you and we love cookies and..."

"My, my, Larry, you're certainly a chatterbox today," said Grandma. "But tell me, where is your sister?"

"Uh...you mean Paulette?

"She's bound to
be here somewhere.
We'll be right back."

The bunny brothers
raced up the stairs, their
hearts pounding.
But Paulette was
sleeping quietly,
curled up with
her bugle.

"At last!" shouted Harry.
"The chance I've been waiting
for!"
He picked up the bugle
and BLEW!

Ta Ta TA! TA TA!   *TA—TA TA TA! TA TA!*

"That was Paulette, Grandma. It's all her fault."
"What on earth do you mean, Harry? I haven't
heard such fine music in years!"

After supper Grandma made a fire and they settled down to wait for Mother Bunny's return.

"We were good little bunnies while she was gone, weren't we, Grandma?" asked Paulette.

"Why, of course, my dear. You're always good little bunnies."